Pilar's Worries

Victoria M. Sanchez
pictures by Jess Golden

Albert Whitman & Company
Chicago, Illinois

To the real Pilar—you are my star!—VMS

To my dear friend Ashley T—JG

Library of Congress Cataloging-in-Publication Data

Names: Sanchez, Victoria M., author. | Golden, Jess, illustrator.
Title: Pilar's worries / Victoria M. Sanchez; pictures by Jess Golden.
Description: Chicago, Illinois: Albert Whitman and Company, 2018.
Summary: Pilar has social anxiety, but when tryouts for her favorite ballet are held she uses the coping techniques she has learned and her love of dance to persevere. | Includes bibliographical references.
Identifiers: LCCN 2018008890 | ISBN 9780807565469 (hardback)
Subjects: | CYAC: Social phobia—Fiction. | Anxiety—Fiction. | Dance—Fiction. | Ballet dancing—Fiction.
BISAC: JUVENILE FICTION / Social Issues / Emotions & Feelings. |
JUVENILE FICTION / Social Issues / New Experience.
Classification: LCC PZ7.1.S2575 Pil 2018 | DDC [E]—dc23
LC record available at https://lccn.loc.gov/2018008890

Printed in China
10 9 8 7 6 5 4 3 2 1 HH 22 21 20 19 18

For more information about Albert Whitman & Company,
visit our website at www.albertwhitman.com.

Pilar pliés while brushing her teeth. Friday is always a good day, a ballet-class day.

She sashays into the kitchen, prepares to leap, and…her feet stop. Auditions for *Winter Wonderland* are Saturday!

Tomorrow? Pilar worries.
I can't dance in front of all those people!
What if I forget the steps?

Pilar lets out her breath. It's her favorite
ballet. She knows all the steps.
    She hugs herself as she enters school. *Pilar,*
she tells herself, *Friday is always a good day.*

But in PE, she drops a
fly ball. She turns pink.

During Library, Pilar
realizes she forgot to bring
her very overdue book.
Her skin prickles hot.

By lunch, her stomach
is squeezed so small she
can only swallow one
bite, even though it's
Pot Sticker Day.

In math, Ms. Jenkins's voice startles
Pilar from her daydream.
"Who would like to solve the problem
on the board?"
Pilar's arm refuses to rise, but
her hand twitches.

"Pilar?" Ms. Jenkins asks.

Pilar immediately forgets the answer.

"Pass," she mutters.

Someone whispers loudly, "She always says pass."

Her eyes tear up. Her
heart beats so fast it
scares her. She panics.
Do I need to go home?

She drops her head…and sees a sticky note
on her desk that says "Breathe." Sebastian,
a friend from ballet, grins. Pilar smiles and
remembers to breathe.

Finally, the last bell. Finally, ballet.
At the studio Pilar's palms touch the warm wood
of the barre, her toes and heels press down on the floor.
Ms. Ward, their instructor, claps. "Let's begin with pliés."

The school day disappears.

After warm-ups, Ms. Ward asks, "Pilar, could you please demonstrate your arabesque?" She sees students staring and Sebastian smiling. Pilar's palms are sticky on the barre but as soon as her leg lifts, her shoulders relax. The rest of the hour breezes by.

"Dancers," calls Ms. Ward, "auditions for *Winter Wonderland* are tomorrow! Please see me if you're interested!"

Pilar's heart leaps! Then her worries creep back.
Should I?

Sebastian signals Pilar, but she turns and packs up.

"Pilar?" It's Ms. Ward. "Signing up?"

"I..." Cheeks burning, she shakes her head.

At bedtime Mama sits on Pilar's bed.
"How was your day, love?" she asks.
Pilar's chest tightens. Then she begins to cry.
"Tryouts are tomorrow, Mama. But I'm too nervous!"
Pilar's mama hugs her. "Whether you try out this year or next year or never, Mijita, you're still an amazing dancer."

"I want to *this* year, Mama, but...my whole body
is scared!"

Mama touches Pilar's chest, their sign for "breathe."

"Mijita, if you decide to audition, you *will* feel scared.
But usually when you are doing what you love, the good
feelings are so big that the bad feelings become small."

Pilar can't sleep. She thinks of *Winter Wonderland* and imagines her favorite part—the dancing snowflakes. She steps out of bed.

Quietly, like nighttime snow, she dances. She feels peaceful and strong.

Tired at last, she collapses into her comforter. "I can do this," she murmurs.

Pilar wakes so early Saturday that she can still see the moon in the violet sky. She pulls her hair into a bun. She makes a snack and fills her water bottle.

Mama walks in, yawning. "Well, good
morning, early bird."
"Mama," Pilar blurts, "I want to audition!"

At the studio, Pilar spies Ms. Ward. Pilar's belly is queasy. She thinks back to dancing last night. She breathes deep. Her teacher smiles.

"Pilar! I am so happy you're here. Everyone's warming up backstage."

Pilar feels like she's swallowed a hundred butterflies
but just as she starts to worry, Sebastian walks up.

"I'm so nervous I want to barf!" he moans.

Pilar laughs and the butterflies float away.

A judge calls, "PILAR!"

The flutters return, but Pilar closes her eyes and breathes deep. *I can do this. This is what I love!* Her legs prickle and her feet feel numb, but she walks to center stage.

The music starts. Pilar closes her eyes and imagines winter and ice. Her flushed cheeks cool. She steps...and dances.

Before she knows it, the music silences and
Pilar walks off stage, beaming and tall.

Next week during Sharing, Ms. Jenkins goes around the circle.

"Pass," says Pilar.

But Sebastian raises his hand. "Pilar and I are going to be in *Winter Wonderland!* We're snowflakes!"

Her classmates speak up all at once. "Cool!" "Wow!" "Whoa!"

Pilar's skin warms, but this time it's nice heat. Like the warmth of a fire after playing in the snow.

A Note from the Author

Pilar's Worries was inspired by my experience watching a child in my family struggle with "the worries" until the day she found her mode of expression through dance. By finding her own method to express herself, she found focus, developed confidence, and discovered courage. And yet her anxiety will never just "go away."

In this book, Pilar uses her "tools"—breathing, positive self-talk—throughout. She also faces a fear that gets in the way of something she really wants. Pilar manages her anxiety in ideal ways, but at the same time, she remains the somewhat reserved child she's always been. In my experience, a significant part of parenting an anxious child is accepting who he or she is, whether shy or outgoing.

There are many children like Pilar. The world is big and they are small. And there's a lot to worry about. Who doesn't remember worrying about test day? Or being startled by fire drills or the news? But when a child's worries become so insistent and overwhelming that they seem too big to soothe, it's time to listen closely. Does the level of worry seem disproportionate to the situation? Does the worry continue even after the situation passes? Is worrying interfering with the important elements of his or her life, like school, friendships, and sleep? Anxiety is the most common diagnosis for children, and it is estimated to affect approximately 10% of all children—but it's also one of the easiest conditions to treat with simple coping strategies and cognitive behavior therapy. With encouragement and family support, things can get a whole lot better.

Selected Resources

Worry Wise Kids (http://www.worrywisekids.org/)
A comprehensive site for all your questions about childhood anxiety. Start here.

Child Mind Institute (https://childmind.org/topics/concerns/anxiety/)
This site focuses on mental health and learning differences in children.

Ronald M. Rapee, PhD, Ann Wignall, D.Psych, Susan H. Spence, PhD, Vanessa Cobham, PhD, Heidi Lyneham, PhD, *Helping Your Anxious Child: A Step-by-Step Guide for Parents* (Oakland, CA: New Harbinger Publications, 2008).
This book has reassuring information, useful activities, and helpful parenting advice.